Clint Faraday
book fifty
Where Death Waits

A man's body is found in the forest in a place no one goes, usually. There is no explanation as to the cause of death.

Those things happen in the Valle de Muerte Esperando. It's not an easy place.

Then another body close to the same area. No cause of death.

It is in the comarca, but neither person was Indio.

Chacho says the people are stupid to go into that forest. It is a place where death waits for victims.

Clint thinks there's more to it than that!

Clint Faraday
book fifty
Where Death Waits
© 2019 by C. D. Moulton

all rights reserved: no part of this publication may be reproduced or transmitted in any form or by any means, electronic or mechanical, including photocopy, recording, or any other information retrieval system, without permission in writing from the copyright holder/ publisher, except in the case of brief quotations embodied in critical articles or reviews.

This is a work of fiction. Any resemblances to persons, living or dead, or events is purely coincidental unless otherwise stated.

<u>Contents</u>

About the author

CD Moulton has traveled extensively over much of the world both in the music business, where he was a rock guitarist, songwriter and arranger and in an import/export business. He has been everything from a bar owner to auto salvage (junkyard) manager, longshoreman to high steel worker, orchid grower to landscaper, tropical fish farmer to commercial fisherman. He started writing books in 1983 and has published more than 350 books as of January 1, 2023. His most popular books to date are about research with orchids, though much of his science fiction and fantasy work has proven popular. He wrote the CD Grimes, PI series, and the Det. Nick Storie series, Clint Faraday series, and many other works.

He now resides in Gualaca, Chiriqui, Panamá, where he writes books, plays music with friends, does research with orchids and medicinal plants. He has lately become involved in fighting for the rights of the indigenous people, who are among his closest friends, and in fighting the extreme corruption in the courts and police in Panamá.

He offers the free e-book, *Fading Paradise*, that explains what he has been through because of the corruption.

CD is the discoverer of the Chadam Protocol for curing cancer.

Facebook page Ambrosia peruviana for cancer.

Clint Faraday, retired (Hah!) PI from Florida, now living in Panamá, took his beautiful young wife and two young children into the large house of Antonio Varellos, a close Indigeno friend who worked with the comarca chiefs in a number of capacities. This was in Buabidi, the capital of the Ngobe Bugle comarca.

Clint, to his great honor, had been declared a Ngobe by the council, the second non-indigenous person ever to receive that honor.

Clint brought the family to Buabidi because they had never been there, except his wife, Tyna. She had come with the wives of a sheik, but that was another story.

It was the short break in the school year in Cusapín, a town in the comarca on the Caribbean where Clint now spent almost half his time. They lived near Quebrada Tula, also in the comarca, much of the time and they had a home in Bocas Town in Bocas del Toro where they spent less and less time. Bocas was too touristy anymore. Clint wanted his children raised in the Indio tradition.

Silvio and Basilio, two chief councilors from the

Caribbean side of the comarca were in town for a meeting of the councilors. Clint had handled a lot of problems in and out of the comarca and was the head honcho of a foundation that was building schools and clinics where needed.

Clint had made, entirely by accident, quite a few millions of dollars through his detective work. He had no use for the money and Manny Matthews (actually Marko Bocinni, a mob boss who had come under a new identity to escape having his children forced to live with how Pops made his. It was Manny's father and grandfather who had run the organization like a mafia mob. Manny had always rebelled against a lot of those practices. He was still among the most powerful mob bosses in the world, but had made the organization go legitimate. The word was spread that he had bought an island in the Mediterranean and was now living there), and Judi Lum, his attractive nextdoor neighbor in Bocas Town, made up the rest of the foundation. Judi was a genius for getting information. She was as much as a partner in the detective business in the past. She handled the financial end of the foundation.

Nito, Clint's son (Clintonito), got out of the car and stretched. He was nine years old. His sister, Nicole, was eight.

Tonio came out of the house to hug them all and

welcome them to his home. He asked Nito what he thought of Buabidi, so far.

"It's a city. I like a puebla. I'm an Indio. People come to cities to look for things that aren't there. Leave that to the Latinos and blacks."

Nito always managed to sound wise and a lot older than he was. Everyone except Tyna, Clint, and he thought he was a genius.

Tonio laughed and said he often wished that a few thousand others thought that way so Buabidi could go back to being an Indigeno settlement.

They went into the house for some snacks, then Nito and Nicole decided to walk around to look over the city. Tonio warned that there were sections in Buabidi that were like sections in Panamá City.

"And every other city. It's why I'll be glad when we go home. I want to know a little about it so I can tell my friends about it."

"I'm glad you don't have some of the problems of big cities," Tyna said. "Clint has enough to do with that crap as it is! Maybe he won't get tied up in some stupid murder, here!"

Tonio laughed. "Well, we don't know if it's murder, and it's not really here. It's just close."

"Don't know?" Clint asked.

"We can't find a cause of death. The dead man wasn't from the comarca. He was a mixed breed from the canal zone. They found him early this morning. I was just consulting with Basilio about it and he said to ask you to help. You know all about murder."

"Where was he found?"

"In the Bosque del Muerte. About sixty kilometers from the city."

"The Forest of Death?"

"It is dangerous. Very few people ever go there. We have no idea why that man went to the forest.

"There are a few very nice spots there, but much of it is very wild. He was found near the Valle de Muerte Esperando."

"The Valley Where Death Waits?"

"The Valley of Waiting Death. Yes. A number of people have died there. At one time there were many of the Lyra Spiders and many snakes.

"It is a beautiful spot, but it is a dangerous spot."

"I guess!"

"Now we have a body. We don't have a cause of death. It was not a spider or snake. There is no sign of violence. The records from the policia say he had no health problems.

"Perhaps there is no need of an investigation. It could well be called a natural death, but we can almost always find the cause very quickly for that. The doctor from the policia can't find why he died. We have a body without a cause, it seems."

Clint sighed and said he would help if he could. It would be nice to get out in the forests. He was like Nito in that!

Clint dismounted from the horse he had ridden the last three kilometers into the forest. It truly was a beautiful, wild place. He was wearing high rubber boots and had sprayed the outer pants with Baygon. He was wearing two layers of clothes. It made it a little warm, but not too much.

Chaco Minas, who found the body, dismounted at the same time. The horses seemed unduly nervous. Chaco said they felt the danger of the place. Animals could sense such things. Clint knew it was a strange smell or a subliminal smell they couldn't detect.

"He was right over there at the start of the trees by the path. He had not been there long. He did not smell of rot. He was laying on his side and I thought he was a stupid who had laid there to sleep where it is very dangerous.

Doctor Gortas had shown Clint the pictures of the place and of the body. They had identification from fingerprints on his passport. He was Dylan Thomas Williams, a man who had been born in the canal zone and who was a dual citizen. His father had been in the US Marines who were stationed there twenty nine years ago, when he was born. His father had married his mother two weeks before he was born. The police were checking on his background. So far, they knew he was born in the zone and had moved to the states when he was six. He lived there nine months of the year and in Panamá three of every year until he finished school in Grand Rapids, Michigan, where his father had a home. He had then spent most of his time in Panamá. He was a master mechanic for a large heavy equipment company and made an excellent living. He often seemed to be living above even that standard. He explained that he was a gambler, a very lucky one. He won a lot more than he lost. He had been living with three different women that people knew of. He had married the first when she, like his mother had been, was pregnant with their daughter. He then divorced her and hadn't married the second one, the mother of his son. He was average popular and didn't have any known serious enemies.

No one had a clue as to why he would be in the wilds in the comarca. He hadn't seemed the type who would enjoy exploring. He was more the city and night life type.

"Why are we here?" Chaco asked.

"There has to be a reason he was here. We won't

find it in Buabidi or in wherever he was living the past few years. It will be something where he was involved with another person. It will probably be something illegal. I think it will have to do with mining. He was working with heavy equipment."

"Then it will be because of the zinc, I suppose. It is not far from here were there is a lot of it, but we mine it with labor, not machines. We do not scar and poison the Earth like the estranjeros."

"You mine it with human labor? Is it that concentrated where you can make a profit?"

"Yes. There are not enough jobs in the city. We have it controlled where they bring in two large carrier trucks every day and we fill them with the best ore. There is only the road and a place that is all rocks of half a hectare where we pile the ore. There is one small front bucket tractor to put the ore in the truck. Tonio can tell you how much they earn with it. It is enough for about a hundred people to feed their families."

Clint knew there were operations of the type, but usually with silver or gold. He didn't really think there was anything like that here, while he couldn't think of anything that would require heavy equipment it could be.

He and Chaco moved along the path into the forest from the point where the body was found. The path led into the mountains in a valley with a small river flowing through. There seemed to be a number of limestone and silica caves in a couple of the sides of the escarpment over the river. A long stretch of the river had very steep banks that went up sharply to the mesa-like mountains on either side.

"I'd say it's something in one or more of those caves. I don't get the need of heavy equipment. Even if there was a tiny gleam of hope of getting permission to bring it there wouldn't be a way to use it here."

Chaco nodded. "Then it is something that some-one told him because he worked with that kind of equipment. Perhaps it is just something that one seeking things that use the equipment would find. I think there is something here." He held up a sliced crystal. It was amethyst. It had excellent color.

"There is a lot of it here?"

"In some of the caves there are large deposits. It is very heavy, and the joyeria store in the city will give us twenty dollars per pound for the regular or thirty five dollars a pound for the good part, like this. When there is an emergency and great need of money three or four of us will come to this dangerous place."

Clint hefted the crystal. "This is about a third of a pound. A sack of a hundred pounds, two of them in a horse pack. Six thousand.

"Is there that much?"

"In the place where I found this there would be a thousand pounds. It is in the walls and is six or eight centimeters thick. It is a long section with mostly very good crystal, though some is not of good color and is not worth the same. I have not been in but two of the caves with the rosada crystals. I am told one farther up has much more that is even better than this, but it is very difficult to go there."

"A thousand pounds would be worth more than half a million dollars. Three caves and you have a million and a half. You could cut it with a diamond saw and carry it out, two hundred pounds per day. Fifteen days for a million and a half. People who are money oriented would find that irresistible!"

Chaco took him to the cave where he got his crystal. It was a fantastic place where he needed a flashlight. It was an amethyst fairyland.

Chaco was wrong about there being a thousand pounds in that cave, though. There were easily two to three thousand pounds. It was slow-formed crystal that had excellent clear color.

They headed back toward the city. Clint had found a spur of the crystal that he could break off. It was about 15CM X 22CM and 5CM thick. It would weigh about six pounds. He estimated a deal could be made with that quality of stone for fifty dollars a pound without any hesitation. He didn't know much about the market, but Dave had found a chunk of amethyst, not of that quality, that a jeweler had given him fifty dollars for. It was a little less than a pound. The jeweler had made a string of beads with a larger heart-shaped pendant that he sold for $900 and hadn't used much more than half the piece.

"We have more than enough motive your honor, and the opportunity was there. We only lack method!"

"What?"

"I was just thinking out loud. You were very wrong about how much there is there and how valuable it would be to an honest jeweler."

Chaco laughed. "I can tell by the fun tone of laughter in your voice that I estimated less in both things."

"Yep! You were about fifty percent too low in both estimates!

"Shall we go back to Buabidi and find a way to keep the greedbags out of here?"

"We agree on many things, my friend."

They went back to Buabidi. Clint went to the joyeria and asked what the raw value of the amethyst would be.

"This quality, I could pay eighty dollars per kilo. If you can find pieces this large, I would suggest you take it to David or Panamá City. I can only pay considering what they will pay me. I do not have the funds here to purchase such large amounts."

"What price could I expect?"

"This is as fine as amethyst gets. It would be worth perhaps three hundred dollars per kilo. Perhaps more."

A hundred thirty five dollars per pound? There really was a fortune in those caves!

Clint thanked him and headed for the hospital. He wanted to see what the doctor had found.

Dr. Gortas was performing lung surgery and wouldn't be available for two hours or more. It was a difficult case. Clint went to the council building and spoke with Tonio and Basilio, who happened to be there for a council meeting. Tonio called in Meri Naomi to explain about the Valle de Muerte Esperando. Naomi was a sort of psychic.

"The legend is that there are caves there under protection of the ancients. They are where the old spirits stayed. The Valle de Muerte Esperando has the protection that those who come there without purpose or with evil purpose will never leave. People who are not of the people will not long survive there. It is a place of the people.

"It is true that the spirits do not directly kill unless there is urgent need. They have things of nature there. The only way the old spirits will intervene is to select who may enter and who may not.

"It is true that this one died of a snake bite and that one was killed by a spider. That snake or spider was put there with instructions by the old spirits.

"In times of real need the spirits will direct one of the people to great treasures. It is a place where there is no gold, yet our people can find it when there is great need. It is a place where there are many jewels, favorites of the spirits, of great clarity and size.

"This is legend from far before the white man came here. It was changed in a vision sent to Mucila Raez when the evil estranjeros were slaughtering the people. The spirits told her to bring the good people to the valley and that they would be safe there, though they must go when the evil has gone. The evil will never enter the valley, or I should say, they will never leave the valley. They and their greeds will perish should they be so stupid as to challenge the spirits.

"Two hundred and twelve of the people went there. They were there for two years and two months and two days. They were all safe.

"The invaders came soon after the people went there. A hundred men and a hundred horses went into the valley. A hundred horses left the valley. The invaders were never heard of nor seen again. There is the story that they had left the horses at the entrance to the valley and had gone into the almost dry river to find where the people were encamped on the other side of the Valley of Waiting Death. There was a sudden great storm of a ferocity that had not been known there and has not been known in the centuries since. The river was suddenly raging and they were in a place where they could not go above the water. None ever left the valley alive. Their corpses were washed into the ocean.

"There are tales of that time in the Spaniards' writings. A storm like they had never known that lasted a mere day and was only in this part of the comarca.

"I know that this man is not the first who has died when there was never an explanation for the death.

"Clint Faraday, be most glad that you are declared of the people. You would not be here now if you were not, though Chaco would also never have taken you there.

"I have been to the valley but once. I could not

stay. The power there is more than I can tolerate, though none of it was directed toward me. I will not again go there."

"Clint, you'll probably consider this a tale made up when a storm killed a bunch of conquistadores at a time when they were killing the people. I am not so sure. I've seen things that have no logical explanation, but that are very real."

"Tonio, I've seen things that would curl your hair. If a natural explanation of the man's death is found, who can say the reason, whatever it was, was even there is that those ancient spirits are very real. They put it there.

"Meri Naomi, I am glad and proud that I am Ngobe."

Naomi nodded and smiled.

Dr. Gortas came into the waiting room a little more than an hour and a half later. Clint, Basilio, and Tonio had gone to get a snack and had just returned.

"I have contacted authorities in David. They will be here for the body in a short while. There is a man they will bring who says he is known to Clint. He studied the paranormal phenomena and has heard of the legend of the valley.

"While I do not accept the explanation of ancient spirits bringing about deaths there I do not reject it. I have heard the stories and have records of two who died there with no reason discovered. I would place this into a probable embolism. I could not and would not accept that every stranger who goes there dies of embolism. It is a relatively rare thing.

"Perhaps the modern laboratories will find what is there, but from the victim. They will not be permitted to go there, I believe.

"That is true, Tonio?"

"For the moment. Clint may change my mind in a special case."

Dr. Gortas had the nurse print out the long list of

tests, all of which were negative.

"There are things that break down in the body after death," Clint suggested. "I think, if this is murder, something such was used."

"Most of them will show damage specific," Gortas replied. "If ingested, there will be traces modern equipment can find. None of those very complicated chemicals would be found in the digestive tract normally. If injected, there will be an injection point. If absorbed, an agent such as EDTA would be used, which we can trace. I've made every test we can make here at this hospital."

Clint nodded. Tonio suggested Clint wait to talk with the person who knew him and who was a paranormal investigator. They agreed to that.

The body was loaded and the test results were given to the driver of the ambulance. The paranormal researcher, Dr. Armitage Lincoln, had checked into the hotel. Clint went to see him at the hospital when he went there to study the tests and reports.

"Mr. Faraday! You will possibly not remember me. I was here for a short time and went to Cusapín to speak with that amazing woman they call Matilde. I was almost to a point where my frustration would cause me to decide the whole bit was fakery and fantasy. (*Dead Zone*) She showed me there was very definitely a power some individuals possess.

"I prattle. I am deeply interested in this. In my studies – I am based in Guatemala, at this time – I had seen mention of this place in a very old record. Fifteen sixties, if I recall correctly. A contingent of conquistadores on horseback went into the area and only the horses returned, none with any sign of damage. None of the soldiers returned, a hundred of them, if the tale can be believed. Their bodies, not one, have not been accounted for to this day!

"Matilde, who corresponds with me at times – a mystic magic woman with a computer! She informed me of this and I came here within the hour! If Matilde says there is a mystery, you can bet the farm, as we say, that there is a mystery!

"I spoke with you at the dock in Cusapín as I was leaving. I thought you were a gringo, but was assured you are Ngobe. I have since learned that you are, indeed, a Ngobe!

"I am most excited! I have studied all the testing procedures, fully expecting to find little gaps and omissions here, as one does not expect a facility in such a place to be, shall we iterate, up to date. Dr. Gortas is a very intelligent and thorough person. I can think of no other test – speaking, of course, of modern medical tests – he has omitted. I am fascinated!

"I must go to this place, Mr. Faraday! I must! I must know why this dead person went there! I must know what happened that would bring the powers down on him!"

"If the legend is true, you would be the next to drop dead there," Clint replied. "We know why he was there. It was basically greed."

"Then I would be safe. I bear no person malice. I don't even understand greed. I am like the Indigenous people in that."

"I'll talk to Tonio and Basilio. Maybe they'll let you go, but it will be with you knowing the risk."

"I accept that. I will sign a statement to the effect with as many witnesses as you like! I want to contact Matilde. My reservation will be that, should she tell me not to go, I would not go."

Clint shrugged and took out his cellular to call Matilde. He put the phone on speaker. She answered, "Coin dere, Clint. Tica Matilde."

"Greetings, Matilde. I am here with Dr. Lincoln. He says you told him about the Valle de Muerte. He wants to go there, but won't if you say he shouldn't."

"He is a strange man. He is very honest and he feels no hatred against anyone nor anything. I will say only that you should go with him and should carry the crystal I gave Tyna. If it gets cloudy, do not proceed farther. Turn back. If it is cloudy to a side, do not go that way. If it is cloudy ahead, do not go farther. If it is cloudy all over, you have big trouble! Go back immediately!

"Clint? If there is a small cloudy spot, it is a place where there is great evil. You may go there, but Army may not. He is to wait until you return. It will be a sign to you alone. He will not see it. If you find the source of the evil, and it concerns Army, you may take him there. It will be a thing to investigate.

"I do not know what is bringing this to me. It will concern you and interest Army. Take the greatest care. There is grave danger there and the spirits wish to warn you!"

"Thank you, Matilde! Army here. This is the most fantastic thing since the death orchid."

"That was resolved? I felt it was not a thing of the dead, but was of the alive and evil."

"Yes! Yes! You said that. It was a man who wanted to make a lot of money or something as crass. Mama Nani unmasked the villain for us!"

"Mama Nani? She has a very small power. I would think she would not aid you with it. You would show all she was of little power."

"She's a good actress. She did it with fakery."

"Fakery! *That* is Nani! I like her, though."

"Do you feel this is real?"

"It is real, but I do not know if it is the ancients or another evil one. It could well be both.

"Naomi lives in Buabidi. Ask her to seek an answer from the spirits that they will allow you."

"Yes! I will do that!"

They chatted for a couple more minutes, then Clint said they would go to Naomi's. If she said it was okay, they would ride out in the morning.

Naomi said he could go to the place where the body was found, but was not to go into the valley farther. Perhaps when the spirits knew his spirit he would be permitted to go farther.

"With the dawn. I'll meet you at the hotel. Don't take much crap. We're coming back before noon."

"A camera and recorder. I'll be waiting."

"Matilde has me wondering. She's never wrong. If she thought there was a lot of danger, she would tell me not to go or tell you not to go.

"I expect something very strange!"

<u>*Number Two*</u>

Clint met Army Lincoln at a quarter to six. As promised, he was in the lobby, waiting. They took a car to the point they would need horses. Lincoln surprised Clint when he was a very good rider. Clint periodically took the crystal out of his pocket to look at it. It seemed to be a quartz crystal, rounded into a bead, and put in a silver setting. Tyna had it in a little ring box.

They were not long before the pleasant little meadow where the body had been found when Clint looked at the crystal. There was a grey spot to their right and slightly ahead. Clint showed it to Army, who saw nothing. He dismounted and said he'd stay right there. Clint headed for the spot that seemed to be indicated on the crystal. There was a man laying beside the narrow animal path. He looked like he was sleeping. Clint dismounted and went to him.

He was dead. He looked like he had simply laid down and gone to sleep. There were no signs of violence or ... anything.

Clint used his satellite cellular to call Tonio. He explained how he found the body.

"Is it in the same place as the first?"

"No, but it's close. Maybe six or seven hundred meters."

"I'll come out and bring a crew. I'll call Doc. He might want to see this one at the scene."

Clint promised to wait. He took out the crystal and saw it was clear. He called to Army, who rode over. He took a lot of pictures, including everything in the close area. He carefully went back along the path, to find footprints in a little muddy spot. They were wet enough that all he could find was the outline and impression, without features.

He looked at them more closely, his brow knitted a moment and he called Clint to show him the prints.

"Clint, they seem to be two different sizes! By very little, like a forty one and a forty two. We can't be sure because of the mud."

Clint nodded and looked along the path.

"I'd say he hasn't been dead more than an hour. Maybe less. We can work from the idea someone came here with him. This is a little too long a stretch to step over and the prints are only in one direction so one went out another way."

"Or in?" Army suggested. Clint nodded.

Clint went back to the main path while Army went on along the path. He came to a coarse rocky area where he knew it would be virtually impossible to check for more, so he headed back to find Clint. They went the short distance to the meadow, where Army took a lot more pictures. He went to the spot the body had been found, but didn't go farther. He felt Matilde had warned him and he would never take what she said lightly.

They heard Tonio coming and met him where Clint first read the crystal to find the body. He had Dr. Gortas and two others with him. Clint explained that both he and Army had a lot of pictures, including the area. There were footprints that may or may not indicate that two people came through. He explained that the mud only took an approximate print. They had not touched anything nor moved anything. Army was more careful than he was with evidence. He wanted everything exact for his own research.

Dr. Gortas carefully checked the body and took his own pictures before turning the body over.

"His identification says he was Jonathon Luis Morales, also a zonie. He was an assay engineer.

"There is no health problem on his card. It's with Central America Comprehensive Health HMO. They would list anything and everything that could even vaguely be considered as pre-existing. I hate dealing with them. I'm glad our people seldom carry such insurance. It is very costly and they refuse to cover anything ... this is not the time for that. It will be very certain he didn't have any health concerns. It is from only thirty months ago so I may rule out embolism that could be this deadly. They would have found it."

He took out a recorder and made all the necessary checks. He said the man had died less than two hours ago of undetermined cause. Time on his watch was nine twenty eight AM on October 13, twenty twelve. He even read the GPS numbers into the record.

"Okay. If we were where it had significance, I would state that we can transport. I'll just ask that Carlos and Naldo pack him into the body bag and we can put him across a horse and get him out. The horses used to transport and to arrive here are the property of Arnaldo Flores.

"Let's get back to town. I have surgery at two. I'll have to be ready."

Tonio said he'd get back now. Clint asked Army if he would like to go back with the doctor and Tonio.

"You will stay?" Army asked.

"I'm going to see if someone went into the valley."

"I may not proceed with you?"

"Not now. We promised Matilde. I don't have the authority or the desire to take you in there."

He showed Army the crystal. It was clouded ahead. Army agreed it would be a terrible idea for him to not trust Matilde.

"Clint, please do not go in there. It bodes evil to you, as well as to me."

Clint stepped to the far side of Army and moved into the meadow. The crystal was still cloudy, but far less than back a couple hundred meters. Army came to look. The crystal clouded decidedly more as he approached. Clint told him that.

"This works like those old mood rings!" Army cried. "We investigated them some years ago, and discovered the ionization of the surface of the skin was able to impart an electrical charge that aligned the molecules to a small degree. It can be done with a static charge, but must be very close. Matilde has discovered a way to make it work at a distance. I was excited to be here and more-so by the discovery of the body, thus I caused the ionization at a distance!"

"And the small spot when I discovered the body?"

"You just couldn't resist knocking my theory over the head, could you?" Army said, with a small chuckle. "I have to remain skeptical to an extreme. I must find any logical explanation I can. If I didn't, I would soon look for proof of the effectiveness of the paranormal answer and would exclude bits. Perhaps I go too far one way, but I feel that it would be better than going too far the other.

"I want very much to prove paranormal powers, but I want that proof to be real. I direct my investigations more to disproof. I have found some proof, anecdotal, such as Matilde. A few things remain with unanswered questions.

"Matilde knows when a woman is pregnant, even if it is only a few days. She knows how the child will be named. That could be a talent or it could be because she stated several names of a vein that would be considered by people she knew. It is natural to remember the times when she seemed to be right and forget the others."

"She told Tyna, my wife, that she was pregnant and that it would be a boy we called Clintonito. We knew Tyna was pregnant then, and if it was a boy the usual naming would be the father's name with the 'ito' ending.

"The next time she said Tyna was pregnant she had been for less than three or four days. Tyna didn't know it. Matilde said it would be a girl, and that we would name her Nicole.

"She couldn't have possibly known that I particularly liked that name. She could have guessed Tyna was pregnant, I suppose. She had a fifty-fifty chance it would be a girl. She couldn't have known about Nicole. I never mentioned to anyone in the country that I liked that name and it isn't a name that would even occur to people here.

"I could have felt she had one lucky guess and that I'd given some kind of hint if that was the only time. I've seen her do it fifteen or twenty times.

"She saw a boat leaving the dock at Cusapín and said that one spirit, the evil one, would not return.

"A woman we all thought was just a normal person died when the parachute she was using, being pulled by the boat, came apart and dropped her onto the rocks. We soon learned that she had truly been an evil person.

"I've never known her to be wrong in any of her predictions. I have seen several times when she was asked something and she said she could get no feeling about it. She would not guess, but it was at least not bad – for that."

"We can discuss this later?" Gortas suggested. "I have to do surgery?"

"Yes. Sorry! I get into my subject and forget everything else," Army said. "I'll see you later, Clint. I urge most strongly that you heed the warnings Matilde has given."

"I'd be a fool not to!"

They left, and Clint mounted up to ride into the Valle de Muerte Esperando.

Clint had learned a lot about tracking a person from his friends in the mountains. He knew where the signs were. He knew the most telling were often the most subtle. A broken twig with ants meant it was very fresh and that the ants were there to get the sugars in the saps. A twig that was broken and had no ants meant it wasn't very recent. He was looking for less than two hours. Any he found with ants might mean someone passed. If he found the twig, he could look on the ground below. If leaves were disturbed or grasses or vines crushed, something heavy had passed. If the broken twig was a meter above the ground, it was not a small animal that had passed there. It was possibly a person. Move to the next clue.

The meadow had to be crossed, but there was little to tell if a person or an animal left a crushed small plant. If there was a probable direction, you searched for footprints or other clues that would not be left by an animal.

In other words, he might not be an expert tracker, but he wasn't a rank amateur, either.

He didn't find much in the little meadow. He

could see where the horses when he and Chaco had come grazed. The grass was already up about four inches. He found another patch that seemed much more recent. Maybe this one had a horse that had gotten free and wandered off. They had been there to retrieve a body not long before. Tracks were already hidden by the grass growth, but were still clear enough to confuse anything more recent.

He dismounted at the start of the path into the valley where the first body was found. Up to that point, it would be difficult to separate new clues from older ones. Beyond that point the clues would be from when he and Chaco went to the caves. He would be able to tell which they left and which someone else left.

The trouble was that there was little there to retain clues.

Wrong! Someone had stopped to clean mud from their shoes by the little stream that would be a river in the rainier times. They had rinsed the shoes in the water and had left mud on the rocks just before the water. The rocks were damp and the mud would be soon washed away, except there was little flow and the mud was in small lumps that hadn't had time to absorb enough water to break down the lumps. It was also not the kind of mud on that bank. It was the redder mud from the flatter places – like where those prints had been found.

Clint could figure this as being the mud caught in the tread of finca boots and on top. The one who left that mud had moved fast to get past the meadow and had stopped in a place that would seem to offer a good way to clean the boots.

That meant an even smaller foot. The body was wearing street shoes, really. They were old and they had the tread worn off. They were size forty two. The others were size forty one, probably. In a finca boot, that would be two sizes smaller than the boots.

Was he following a woman? Forty two was a fairly small foot. These were smaller yet.

Clint tied the horse where it could reach fresh grass and moved silently into the forest path. The trail was a lot easier to follow where it was so restricted. It had to go along the riverbed.

Twenty minutes later Clint reached the first of the caves. There was no indication anyone had come there. Perhaps the person had gone directly to the second cave. Chaco said that one was a little better than the first and the one higher was better than either of the two near the river.

He moved cautiously toward the second cave. He spent a few minutes exploring around it, but didn't find anything that would indicate anyone passed there. Surely no one would attempt to climb to that third cave! Clint wouldn't attempt it unless there was someone else along! If he fell or slipped, as seemed likely, he would want someone who could come to his aid.

He went to a little knoll by the river to look back along the way he had come. Where would anyone be able to leave the trail?

There were little seams and rifts, but they were dead ends. No one would ... unless he had been spotted. Someone could slip into a cleft and he would go right past them.

He moved as far to the side as he could to get a view of the river bed he had followed.

Just at the end of his view, where the river went around a bend, he saw a flash of bright yellow. Some birds flew out of a little copse and screeched, then went back after half a minute.

Clint went as fast as he could to the river and downward toward the bend, but knew it would be much too late to catch anyone before the meadow.

He finally reached the meadow to find what he feared had happened. His horse was gone. His quarry would ride out and he would have to walk out. He had been outfoxed.

No sense in delaying. He started out at as fast a trot as he could maintain without tiring.

He found his horse grazing in a small grassy spot

five hundred meters from the road. He took the horse back to Arnaldo Flores' finca. He called a taxi and waited. He asked if there had been any other taxis out since Tonio and crew left. There hadn't been. Naldo hadn't seen anyone else around. No one had come out of there that way.

He considered, then asked Naldo to keep the taxi there when it came. He would be right back.

He took the horse to ride back to where it had been grazing. There was nothing obvious there.

He went farther up the trail and found where someone had gotten off the horse and gone into the forest, about a hundred meters before the grassy spot.

He very carefully went into the dense forest and followed the obvious trail. Whoever went in there wasn't trying to keep from being detected.

There was a little ditch not far into the forest. Clint went to it. There was nothing to indicate anyone crossed the almost dry ditch, meaning they would have gone along it. They would be headed toward the road. Left. He moved the scrub aside that was hanging over the ditch and took a look.

He sighed, and took out his cellular.

"Tonio? Clint. I'm at a little quebrada a couple hundred meters from Naldo's finca. There's a woman's body about ten meters from me. I was tracking her in the valley. She must have spotted me. She doubled back and got my horse. I had to come out on foot. The horse was just past here. There was no one on it. No one came by Naldo's. I rode back to see if someone had used the same trick to evade me a second time.

"I found where she got off the horse and came into the forest to the ditch. I came in and found her.

"There were Lyra spiders near where the horse was tied. I'd say she was bitten twice, minimum. She has that color and the bloated spots on her arms. She must have been almost unconscious and in a lot of pain when she got or fell off the horse. She ran in here and died."

"Of spider bites, not a curse!" Tonio replied.

"Unless the curse is why the spiders were there?"

"Her name was Ana Little. She was another zonie," Tonio reported. "She was the recording secretary of the same mining company where Morales was doing contract discovery work. They're listed in several countries and have made a go of finding small lodes and veins of a number of things. They sometimes find things that take heavy equipment, such as a coal mine in Colombia and a cinnabar lode in Nicaragua. They've found silver and tin and zinc and copper. They found emeralds and sapphire in Colombia, and a good bit of lead in Paraguay.

"They send people like Morales and Williams and her to locate things from mixing with the locals in an area and following up on the tales. Sometimes that can pay off. It would have here if it wasn't on the comarca."

"They found the amethyst and figured it was something they didn't need to split with the company," Gortas suggested.

"Then they decided they didn't need to split with each other, either," Clint said. "That's what we're supposed to think."

"What did I miss?" Tonio asked.

"Where is whatever she supposedly used to kill Morales? A container, empty or not?

"There's someone else. I don't know if that one meant for her to die. That could be spiders. The someone else would want to use the same thing used on Williams and Morales to keep it in the curse framework.

"I think we'll have to see who asks questions about Little. They won't have any about the other two. They know everything they need to know about that.

"You've found where they were staying here?"

"Williams and Morales were at the Tigre," Tonio replied. "Little, we're trying to find. I think we'll find the important answers because of her."

They agreed she was probably the key.

"I'll move around and try to find where she was staying. It wasn't in the main part of Buabidi or you'd already know. Doc will have to get back to work and you can contact everywhere close. Between here and David. The council has the cooperation with the police in that kind of thing," Clint suggested.

They agreed. Clint went to the house to spend some time with his family. Nito and Nicole had made friends with several kids their age. Tyna had seen enough of the city. They all wanted Clint to finish this mystery stuff so they could go back to Cusapín.

"I think, if I can find where Ana Little was staying, I can trace this pretty fast. It might turn out to be one of those odd things we won't ever be able to prove one way or another."

"Was she that woman who was staying at Dario's place?" Nito asked.

"Dario's place?"

"Yeah. Dario Castillo's. She was here from Caracas or somewhere. Dario's papa knew her from when they knew each other in the zone. They hung out a lot and had some kind of deal for a company or something. Dario says her two friends ... that's right! She was a zonie! Her friends were from Caracas! Dario said they wouldn't even be here if his papa wasn't Ngobe."

"Son, I think I have to talk with Dario's papa! Where is their place?"

"It's toward the east, three kilometers. He has a place where he grows corn part of the year. I can take you there. We went once. Yesterday."

Clint nodded and said they'd grab a taxi.

"Why not take our own car?" Nito asked.

Clint laughed. "Because I forgot we drove here! Let's go!"

The whole family would go. It was a beautiful area and was out of town.

They saw a boy of about Nito's age walking toward town. Nito said that was Dario, so they stopped and took him aboard. He said those two men who knew Tia Ana were there. His father was arguing with them because they wanted to get some business papers or something from Ana's room. They said she was dead and they had to have the business papers. Harry, Dario's father, said to get the council to say it was alright.

The drove into the neat little farm and to the house, where Harry was arguing with two men. Clint went to them and introduced himself. Dario knew Clint was working with Tonio and Basilio and said Clint could give the council permission.

"I'm Julio Comacho and this man is Andres Restrepo," one of the men said. "Ana Little was working for a company we own. All we want is the business papers she had."

"So? Ask her for them. If you're entitled to them, she'll give them to you."

"She's dead!" Restrepo cried.

"Well, a death certificate to show the council and it's done."

"She only died this morning. We don't have any death certificate," Comacho replied. "All we want is a contract and the reports from two others she had."

"Get the reports from the two others and present

a death certificate. You're business people, but don't know how to run a business?"

"They reported to her," Restrepo said. "She had their reports."

"So? Tell them to file new ones. They do work for you?"

"They did. They're dead, too," Comacho said. "It's just a few sheets of paper, for god's sake!"

"Two are dead? The two from the Valle de Muerto Esperando?"

"Yes! They reported to her, she kept the records and reported to us."

"She's dead, too? She died at the valle?"

"Yes!"

"How did you know she died this morning at the valle? That information hasn't been released."

"A man told us. He works for the police and was there to get her body." Apparently Restrepo was going to do the talking, now. He'd given Comacho a scorching look at that last outburst.

"Oh? Which one?"

"Which one what?"

"Which person who works for the police told you?"

"We just call him, uh, Sam."

"There was no Sam there. How did he tell you?"

"A phone call! My dear god!" Comacho cried, getting another hard look. Harry looked interested and amused.

"I see. A man who wasn't there called you on a phone from a dead signal area to report that Ana Little was dead.

"How did he know it was her?"

"From the police!"

"A man who wasn't there called you on a phone from a dead signal area to tell you a woman who wasn't identified until and hour ago was dead. That would almost fit the legend of the valle!"

Harry, Nito, and Dario laughed. The rest of the family was at the house, talking with Harry's wife, or they would have joined in the laughter.

"We want those legal papers, and we want them right now!" Restrepo demanded.

"We all want things we can't have, at times. Kiss my ass," Clint replied, calmly. "You two have a lot of explaining to do. You are charged, at this moment, with murder, separately or together. You can come into town or we can take you into town in restraints. Your choice."

"We didn't kill her! It was a spider!" Comacho cried. "She was a partner! She knew where it was!"

"Everybody in the area knows where it is. The murders are Williams and Morales."

"Yeep! We didn't kill anybody! She might have," Restrepo yelled. "They died of the curse!"

"Yet you went back there?"

"She went back, not us!" Comacho said.

"Oh? That was a ghost on a horse in broad daylight?"

"A horse?" Restrepo asked, giving Comacho another look.

"In the meadow where Ana went into the valle. Yes. A horse."

"Julio? That really was Soltero I saw you talking to in David?

"Don't lie to me now!"

"I swear! He was supposed to follow them is all! I didn't know he would kill them! He was working for Ana, not me!"

"A man named, so far as we know, Santo Soltero, was in the company a few months ago. We did not approve of his methods and expelled him," Restrepo said. "Apparently, Ana was still working with him."

"You didn't approve of his methods, yet you came here to steal the amethyst that belongs to the people here? Really?" Clint asked.

"He is an animal! A brute! He beats people. He has even killed people!" Comacho cried. "He said he would kill me if I told Andres he was here!"

"Let's go into town. I think the council will want to know about this Santo character," Clint said. "Nito, tell Tyna I'll be back for you as soon as I can."

"Okay. I think we'll walk back with Dario. It's nice, and we won't be back there for awhile."

"Call me if you want me to come after you," Clint said. He waved to the car and he and Restrepo and Comacho got in to drive into Buabidi.

"Give Tonio a very complete and a very clear statement and you may possibly go," Basilio ordered Restrepo and Comacho. "It will be for Clint to decide. We had turned this over to his authority, and will abide by his decision. We will video-record the entire session. We do not depend upon papers to a great extent here. Be aware that you are not under Panamanian law here. This is the comarca.

"Clint, it is now your responsibility. We will leave the room should you so desire."

"This is comarca concern. You're the council. You should stay.

"Let's just get your combined statement as to what happened, from the start. I'll ask questions when I think they're needed.

"Which one speaks first? The other can confirm or deny when the statement's finished."

Restrepo said he would explain basically what had happened. Clint could ask anything that needed clearing up.

"It started fifteen years or more ago. In the canal zone. A man from here was working on the canal locks and we were management on the project.

"The man, Harry Castillo, has a large and very high quality block of amethyst. He told tales of the place it is found and said there are literally tons of the stuff in caves in the area. He said no one goes to where it's found because of an old protection by the ancient spirits. Anyone who goes there with evil intent or who is not of the native people will die there. It is even called the valley where death waits.

"The man, Harry, stayed for a couple of months with a woman named Ana Little. He told her even more of the tales.

"Harry returned to Buabidi, his home. We stayed in contact about once a year. He had married and had a family, a son. He has a large home and we would visit the last three years. He took us to the road just before the valle of death and said the caves with the amethyst were there.

"Two years ago we came not long after a man had been found in the valle. There seemed no reason for him to have died. The people related tales of many who entered the valle and never returned or were found dead there. There was seldom a cause of death, but some died of snakebite or spider bite. The story was that the spirits directed the snakes or spiders to kill.

"We were shown several more pieces of amethyst. We had believed what we had seen was as fine a quality as existed. Some was, hard to believe! better!

"Ana was working with a man called Santo Soltero. We formed a company separate from the company we already worked with as directors. We could use the contacts from that company to move large quantities of amethyst at top prices.

"It was only to find a way to mine the stone. Ana had that plan using Harry, who never suspected anything like this.

"Soltero was intimidating people. He related that he had once worked as a professional money collector for drug dealers from Colombia, had even killed some people. He threatened us. We expelled him from the company.

"We put our plan into effect just last week. We came for a visit with Harry. Dylan and John would stay in the hotel, and would gather the stone. They would leave the stone with us at Harry's. We would send it out with items we would purchase here. It would be stored in David until we had two hundred fifty pounds. We had been assured that much was easily available. Our buyer would, if we kept the quality that we had shown him, pay us three hundred forty dollars per pound. That is seventy five thousand dollars we could collect in just three days. We could arrange for any amount if, indeed, it was here. We estimated we could get as much as a million dollars worth in less than a year.

"Dylan was found dead at the head of the valley. There was no cause of death found. Ana wanted to continue, as did John. Julio was skeptical, and I was very nervous. I have seen things in the canal zone among the voodoo people that is not explainable.

"We decided to proceed with extreme caution. John went to find the stone. John was found, by yourself, dead, with no cause of death.

"Julio and I decided we would not go further with what has become a terrifying situation. Ana had insisted she would follow John and would see what happened. She said there had to be someone there, that people didn't drop dead without cause. That was all scare stories.

"Now Ana has died. We wanted to get our contracts and anything that tied us to the dead people and go.

"Now I find that Soltero is here. I'm not so sure a curse had anything to do with it. I feel we have unknowingly involved ourselves with a coldblooded killer!"

"It is not a curse. It is a protection," Basilio said. "The snakes and spiders can be directed by the spirits. So can people. The protection has never failed and will never fail. People who go there for the good of the people or in need of help are never harmed in any way. The jewel is taken and the person returns to use it in a way that is for the good of the people.

"I have much studied this. When there is good purpose, the stone presents itself. If a piece is dislodged or cut, there will be no scar. It will regrow the missing part. Many people have a small bit that was cut from the first cave.

"Should you be worthy and go to the cave you will find no scar. You will not find where the bit was taken."

Clint thought about it. It was true. He found noplace any had been taken, yet Chaco had a piece that had been cut from that cave. It was also true that the piece he had given Tyna was sticking out like it was being offered!

There was something that was more important than the legends, now.

"Do you have anything to add now?" he asked Comacho, who shook his head.

"Very well. Where will we find Soltero?"

They didn't know. Ana was apparently in communication with him. Maybe in her papers.

Clint said, "I'll be back. An hour!" and got up to race for his car.

Clint jumped out of the car and raced toward Harry's house. Nito and Dario came from around back and asked what the problem was.

"Has anyone come around asking you anything about the woman?" Clint asked.

"No. We're back by the stream," Nito said.

Clint went around and down to the little stream. Harry had a table under a large tree. They were sitting around, talking.

"Harry, may I have your permission to search Ana's room?"

"Yes. Whatever you like. You will want to take her things to town. Perhaps she has relatives who will want them."

Clint went back to the house with Dario and Nito, who would show him which room Ana used. There wasn't much there, but there was a laptop computer and a satchel/valise with pictures and contracts. Clint gathered it all and said that a man would probably come who would want her things. He was to be told, "Mr. Soltero, everything is gone. The council has it." No more.

"What if it isn't Mr. Soltero?" Nito asked, innocently.

"He may not be using that name, but it will be

Soltero."

He took the items to his car and wondered: Why hadn't Soltero already been there? Where was he?

He drove back to town. They checked the computer, to find that she had been corresponding with a1stlonelyalone 1@xyzmail.com. It was mostly about what she was finding and what she planned. Nothing definite. She had received a phone number in an early message. Clint called it, but there was no answer. Only "call failed" came on the screen. His cellular was either off, discharged, or in an area where there wasn't a signal.

He checked the rest of the computer. She had carefully refrained from putting anything on it that would tell anyone anything.

Where was Soltero? Why hadn't he come for those papers? Did he know that she hadn't left anything that could be used?

Had he decided to go into the valley after the amethyst, himself?

That would fit. No signal for the phone. It would fit the type he was, too.

Clint sighed and made a call: "Hi, Army. Want to go find the latest victim of the Valle de Muerto Esperando?"

Clint and Army went slowly along the trail to the meadow. The crystal didn't cloud, so they tied the horses and went on foot into the river bed. After about a kilometer Clint thought he saw a tiny gray spot on the crystal, far to the right. He turned that way and soon came to a cleft. Here were signs someone had come that way.

He checked the crystal. The spot was dead ahead and had grown. There was no indication Army was to be excluded this time. They went on. Soltero's body was laying against a large rock. He was bloated and staring.

"Fer de lance," Army said. "Another evil person has met his end in the valle. We have evidence that there are a lot of poisonous snakes of the most deadly kind here, yet I feel ... safe.

"Another instance where I can't prove nor disprove psychic interference. It's very strange to always be in a position where what I seek is indeterminate in such a...."

Clint's satellite phone buzzed. He answered. It was Matilde.

"Leave it!" She rang off.

"Well, I'd call that a true psychic experience!" Clint said.

"What? What happened?"

"It was Matilde. She said to leave the body here."

"I can see why she ... How did she know? We just got here!"

"As I said, a true psychic experience. Let's go the hell back to Buabidi."

"Would it be alright if I went to a cave first?"

Clint nodded. "There's something I want to check, myself."

"What?"

"Where some of the amethyst was cut from a cave wall."

"Yes. That will tell you how thick the deposit is and possibly how long they have been taking it."

"Something like that."

They went to the cave and checked it carefully. There was no sign anything had ever been taken from the cave.

"Maybe they take it from one of the others?" Army asked.

"They say not. I think that's for you." He pointed to a little blade of very good quality amethyst sticking out from a large crystal cluster. Army touched it to check the color and it fell out in his hand. He had a very surprised look on his face, then a smile.

"Thank you!"

They explored a little further. Clint felt, as did Army, that they were welcomed in that place.

After about an hour and a half they headed back to Buabidi. Clint's family was back at Tonio's and were more than ready to go back to Cusapín. Clint was with them in that! They would leave in the morning.

"You are leaving here before we find Soltero?" Tonio asked.

"According to Matilde, he won't be found. He's dead," Army said. "I believe he discovered that the valley where death waits was not the place for a person of his type. It is a place for good people.

"Clint said you could allow the two surviving to leave the comarca. I think that would be a wise decision."

"Yes. They are as much as cursed here," Basilio said. "I can understand why they are alive. They never went to the valley. If Matilde says he is dead, his body is in the valley somewhere. It can rot there.

"Army, have you found your true magic here?"

"Not from the valley. I did find what I feel is irrefutable proof of at least some people having a psychic power."

"Where did you find that proof?"

"In the valley, but not of the valley."

"You are like Clint. You don't make sense. What do you mean? How did you find it?"

"Clint's phone." He grinned at the confused look on Basilio's face. "Clint got a call from Matilde when we found something. It was just as we found it. She's in Cusapín. It wasn't possible for her to know. She called, knowing all about it."

"Ah! So you did find Soltero's body!"

"We found this." He took the amethyst blade from his backpack.

"You, a stranger, a gringo, not of the people, took that from the cave ofthe spirits – and are still alive?" Basilio asked with a grin.

Meri Naomi, who was sitting at the table with Tyna, said, "In his heart, he is of the people. He is a good person. He is equal with us. He admires those who deserve admiration. He is much like Clint."

"Naomi, how did Matilde know what we had found?" Army asked. "How does that crystal work?"

"Crystal?"

"She gave me a crystal to warn of any danger," Tyna answered for him. "It has clouded spots in the direction of danger."

"You were using the crystal?"

"Yes. Clint had it."

"It told her."

"Which is still the strong psychic ability," Army agreed.

"It is what you call it. To us, it is a talent she was born with. Some have flat noses, some have fine noses. Some have big feet, some have small. Some know things about what is there, some do not. Some can sing, some cannot."

"Well, I would like to stay here for awhile, but in the mountain villages, not in a city. I seldom find what I study in cities. You are an exception.

"I guess that can never be. It *is* the comarca."

"The ancients have accepted you and you carry a piece of their home to show that acceptance. You are welcome anywhere on the comarca," Basilio said.

"Really? I can stay? I can go to places like Quebrada Tula or Loma Yuca or Tobobé?"

"You are welcome. You know of Tobobé?"

"Yajaira was telling me about it and about their medicine woman. She can touch you and know exactly what problems you have with health issues. She can directly cure only a few things, but knows which plant will cure you.

"She is a delightful person. She is beautiful and smart."

"I would see you together. I would know if you are fated."

"Oh! I mean ... well, I'm certainly attracted to her, but I'm forty seven years old and she's only about twenty!"

"And?" Tyna asked. "Clint's seventy and I'm twenty four!"

"Seventy?! I thought about sixty, outside!"

"Age is a number," Tonio said. "There are many instances where numbers are only numbers, and don't mean anything."

<u>*Back to Normal*</u>

Clint laid back in the hammock and tousled Nito's hair. They were back in Cusapín, and glad to be.

Matilde came walking along the beach and waved a greeting. Tyna saw her and went to walk with her to chat. Nicole said it was time to go to school. Nito got up and put on some clothes, then he and Nicole went up the beach toward the school in town.

It was time for him to go to work. Today he was digging yuca to take to Chiriqui Grande for the market. Tomorrow he was going with Omar to get conch and lobster. He would help finish the new council house the following day.

He got a call from Judi Lum, in Bocas Town, asking if she could get six hundred thousand from the account to make the final payment on the large hospital they were constructing near Quoronte. She, Manny Mathews, and Clint spent most of the millions he had made (mostly by accident) with the detective work in building hospitals and clinics and schools on the comarca. He explained for the thousandth time that she didn't need his approval. She was in charge of the project money. It was needed. Use it. It wasn't any use sitting there in the bank.

He dressed for the dirty job and went to the community yuca farm area. Estefan gave the orders of which to dig. It was perfect!

Digging yuca isn't an easy job. Clint had many millions in the bank, and could hire someone to do any of that kind of work, but he was a Ngobe, so would do the work. Without that, he had no purpose in life. A person needed a place and purpose. He and his family all had that!

Clint's nutty musician/botanist friend, Dave, came to ask what had happened with the ghost thing in Buabidi. Clint told him and said it wasn't ghosts.

"Ancient spirits in a cave aren't ghosts?"

That got him the finger.

Selma, Dave's steady ladyfriend (when they were in the same town, which was hardly ever, anymore) came to chat for a few minutes. They soon left. Dave was going into the interior of the comarca.

"Near Tobobé?" Clint asked.

"Around that area. Nobody's ever done any classification in a few thousand square kilometers around there."

"Say hello to Army for me if you see him."

"Okay. Who in hell is Army?"

"Armitage Lincoln, psychic researcher."

"Oh. Married that Yajaira girl? Beautiful and smart?"

"Did he? He was thinking about it."

Dave left. Clint finished the day with a feeling of accomplishment. He got home and went swimming with the family for a half hour, then they went to the house.

"Matilde says she knows the poison Soltero used on Williams and Morales. It's something the drug dealers in Colombia extract from the plant that's such a good abortive."

"That's a form of estrogen. I was right in thinking it had to be one of those things that are found in the body, anyhow, but that break down fast."

"It makes you very tired and you lay down. Your heart stops beating. You die."

"Well, that makes it something not from the valle spirits."

"Unless they caused that Soltero person to use it. He and the Ana woman had been to the valle before, or almost. They didn't actually go into the valle, except that last time. The snake and spider could have been put there by the spirits.

"Clint, Williams and Morales hadn't actually

done anything. They only planned to. Little and Soltero were evil, and did things. The spirits might have brought the end of their schemes to them."

"Yes. Army says that might have happened.

"Or not."

"Are you going to Chiriqui Grande with Omar tomorrow?"

"Yes."

"We need sugar and rice."

"Okay."

C. D. Moulton's works are available on most major outlets as printed or e-books. CD writes the CD Grimes, PI, mysteries, the Det. Lt. Nick Storie mysteries, the Clint Faraday mysteries, the Flight of the Maita science fiction series, books on orchid culture and many others of many types. Mystery, adventure, intrigue, science fiction, humor, fantasy, paranormal, mild erotica, and factual.